Leningrad's Ballet

Rossi Street.

Leningrad's Ballet

Maryinsky to Kirov

John Gregory and Alexander Ukladnikov

Robson Books

AUTHOR'S NOTE

Inevitably there are artists and dancers who have contributed to the Kirov's tradition and history who have not been caught in the focus of our lens and whose names do not appear in these pages. This omission is no reflection upon their status, but is occasioned by the limited scope of the book, which is not a history but a tribute, with the spotlight picking out just some of the outstanding artists past and present.

The pictures by Sasha Ukladnikov have captured memorable moments, and something more, exemplifying not only the glories of the classical dance, but the ever recurring freshness of youth, the inner core of discipline, the pervading grace, and perhaps a glimpse of the intrepid soul of Leningrad. For some, these pictures will evoke treasured memories, for others they will provoke insatiable curiosity. As they stand they may be enjoyed for their intrinsic merit.

JOHN GREGORY

The author wishes to record his thanks to Natalia Dudinskaya and Konstantine Sergeyev for their contributions and help; also to Mary Leitch and Elizabeth Rose for editorial assistance, to Jean Goodman for separating the author from the book, to the British Council for assistance in negotiating visits to cultural institutions in the USSR, and to Jeremy Robson for his courage, insight and skill in publishing the book.

FIRST PUBLISHED IN GREAT BRITAIN IN 1981 BY ROBSON BOOKS LTD., BOLSOVER HOUSE, 5–6 CLIPSTONE STREET, LONDON W1P 7EB. COPYRIGHT © 1980 JOHN GREGORY AND ALEXANDER UKLADNIKOV.

Book designed by Stonecastle Graphics

British Library Cataloguing in Publication Data

Gregory, John,
    Leningrad's ballet.
    1. Kirov Ballet School – History
    I. Title   II. Ukladnikov, Alexander
    792.8′07′04745   GV1788.6.L46

ISBN 0–86051–110–3

Printed in Hungary

Contents

'*Ulanova is ethereal. It's difficult to know how else to describe her. She is thistledown on the stage, passing across it as breath; she floats. There will only ever be one Ulanova . . .*

The gods have given something to Ulanova beyond conception; though a life of dedicated hard work is behind her, she has an extra gift of purity which cleans us all out . . . after a performance by Ulanova you don't feel the same . . . a very chaste ecstasy settles inside . . . it is the purity of it . . .

Ulanova is pure dance.'

HAROLD ELVIN, *The Gentle Russian*

Head of Apollo in the gardens of Pushkin – formerly Tzarskoi Selo.

Genesis

Leningrad: the last centre of civilized elegance, built on the edge of arctic seas and frozen swamps – surrounded by lakes and silent forests – standing in the purity of whiteness . . . White is the colour of classical ballet, the symbol of its purity. It was no accident that the classic dance adopted St. Petersburg (Leningrad) and sprang to life in this white citadel of culture. It was placed there by fate, by royal command, and it took root . . .

Classical ballet: the human architecture of anatomy synchronizing with the movements of artistic evolution – a marrying of the ancient classicism with Gothic mystery and austerity, with the related curves of the Rococo, with the embellishments of Baroque, and finally with the otherworldliness of Romanticism. All art is a blending of elements, derivative strands and fine shades of feeling, a refining of substance towards a summit of expressive truth, an undeniable truth, a supra-human truth.

One thinks of the personality of Leningrad, inevitably linking it with the past – the nostalgia of St. Petersburg, aristocratic city, élite centre of the arts and capital of social graces, weathering all climates, all changes. Today, as second city of the USSR, Leningrad retains its regal dignity despite the transfer of power, despite political demotion. Its ancestry and long tradition are the hallmarks of its greatness. A noble city of fair aspect; yet sad, deeply sad; too much rent by the ravages of history. The wounds heal, but the scars remain. That deep-lying sadness and tragic mien contribute to the heroic edifice – great ballet!

Ballet in its finest mantle is really the summit of human discipline. Ballet has long been the heart and core of Leningrad, the symbol of its impregnable strength, and its unassailable beauty.

Vaganova Choreographic Academy, Rossi Street.

The Evolution of the School

'Russian ballet began with twelve little girls,' said Tamara Karsavina. How small was that beginning! It happened because the Empress Anna was fond of dancing and pageantry. Under Peter the Great the dance had developed socially, but Anna took things a step further. Not content with having amateurs and foreign artists performing, she instituted a ballet school on the attic floor of the Winter Palace in St. Petersburg in 1738. Young girls were chosen from amongst the palace menials, and a nanny was assigned to them. The French ballet master Jean Baptiste Landé was brought from Paris to give instruction. Very soon classes in classical ballet were introduced into the naval cadet school so that the girls would have dancing partners.

Hermitage Theatre in the Winter Palace – the private theatre of the Imperial Family where ballet performances were sometimes given.

9

A few years later the ballet master pronounced his pupils fit to appear on the stage. It was the first corps de ballet to be seen in Russia, the first body of dancers to perform before an audience – the prototype of modern ballet.

The Empress Elizabeth, a Junoesque beauty who ascended to the throne in 1741, was passionately fond of dancing, and during her reign French and Italian ballet masters presented ballet and opera in the Court festivities. The Italian master Antonio Fusano introduced the Commedia dell'Arte as well as subjects from Greek and Roman mythology.

The Russians took to dance with a joyous intensity; they endowed it with gusto and flair. A great ballerina once said, with more than a grain of truth, 'Scratch a Russian and you find a Tartar.' At any rate they showed a natural aptitude that surpassed normal talent. Their physique and temperament were highly charged, and they were able to infuse the classical style with their own rich layers of folk dance. Their spontaneous and instinctive feeling for carriage and *épaulement,* their agility and style, emanated from this source.

From its earliest beginnings Russian ballet has always been subject to outside influences. It was reared and nourished from European culture. During the 1760s Franz Hilferding came from Vienna with a troupe of dancers which enjoyed remarkable success and opened the eyes of the Russians to improvements in style and taste. Hilferding produced ballets using both his own troupe and Russian dancers. By this means the French-trained Russians were able to assimilate a broader conception of the new art of ballet and to make continuous progress.

Under Catherine the Great the development of ballet went forward with more importations of ballet masters: Charles Le Picq from France, and Gasparo Angiolini from Italy. By the end of the century when Paul the First was on the throne, the Imperial Theatres had been established as a State system under a directorate set up by Catherine's decree. From now on the professionalism of ballet under Court sponsorship was secure.

The first Russian ballet master to make a name was Ivan Valberg, a man of artistic discretion as well as a fine teacher. His family name was Liesogorov, but possibly because of the prestige of imported ballet masters, he chose to be known by the foreign-sounding name of Valberg. He produced many notable ballets, including some patriotic pieces during the time of the Napoleonic Wars.

With the dawn of the nineteenth century Charles Louis Didelot (1767–1837), a Swedish-born dancer and choreographer of international fame, came to St. Petersburg. He had received most of his training from Dauberval and Vestris in Paris and brought with him many choreographic refinements. Said to be a man of fiery and unpredictable temperament, he nevertheless spent two long periods in Russia (from 1801 to 1811 and 1816 to 1837), creating spectacular ballets of exceptional charm. One of his ballerinas, Avdotia Istomina, a fey, ethereal creature, is immortalised in Pushkin's verses from *Eugene Onegin*;

> *. . . The rustling curtain has gone up!*
> *And there, resplendent, in the middle,*
> *Sways to the music of the fiddle,*
> *Istomina, her bevy there*
> *Surround that creature, half of air.*
> *First with one foot the floor she brushes,*
> *And on the other slowly twirls,*
> *Then swiftly leaps, and swiftly whirls*
> *Like down by Eolus puff'd, and rushes,*
> *And coils, uncoils again — how quick*
> *Her little feet together click!*

Avdotia Istomina.

Didelot was aided by the French virtuoso Duport, who also contributed to the choreography. The young ballerina Marie Danilova fell in love with the sensational Duport, and it is said that when he left Russia she died of a broken heart. Didelot departed to enjoy successful seasons in London and Paris, but later returned to St. Petersburg to further enrich the ballet.

It is recorded that towards the end of his life Didelot received harsh treatment at the hands of Prince Gagarin, director of the Imperial Theatres. In spite of this he left his property to the State to found a scholarship fund for talented young dancers in the school.

Another important factor in the evolution of Russian ballet was the publication of the letters of George Jean Noverre, the French ballet master whose dictums revolutionized ballet technique, and who introduced the *Pas d'Action*. He was the first ballet master to bring an awareness that technique was only the means; that without artistry technique was but an empty vessel.

This was further demonstrated by the great Marie Taglioni.

Anna Prikhunova.

Departure of girls of the theatre school from the stage-door of the Alexandrinsky Theatre, circa 1839. From a watercolour by N. S. Apolonskaya.

Marie Taglioni.

Making her debut in St. Petersburg in 1837 with *La Sylphide*, she continued to visit Russia annually during the next six years, enjoying phenomenal success in her father's ballets which were tawdry vehicles thrown together to exploit her inspirational charm. Undoubtedly she influenced the ballerinas of the day with her ethereal qualities; it was said that 'she danced as nightingales sang'. Thus then, as now, the development of dance was influenced more by personalities and individual artists than by the system of schooling, which had not yet matured.

After the reign of Didelot came Jules Perrot and the blossoming of the great Romantic era which was to last right into our own century. Perrot was born in Lyons in 1800 and was a pupil of Vestris, the acclaimed 'God of the Dance'. He came to St. Petersburg in 1848 and in 1851 received the official title of ballet master. The creator of *Giselle* and *Esmeralda*, he was a man who worked from inspiration; consequently there were periods of total inactivity and frustration, and by all accounts whole days would sometimes go by at rehearsals without a single step being created. Nevertheless his ballets became classics, and he was much loved and respected by Russian dancers and public alike. His favourite ballerina was Anna Prikhunova, the wife of Prince Gagarin.

During the ensuing period ballerinas of such international repute as Carlotta Grisi, Fanny Elssler and Lucille Grahn were guest artists at the Maryinsky (the system of guest stars was similar to that operating in the West today), but at the same time home-bred ballerinas such as Yelina Andreyanova, Anna Prikhunova and Tatiana Schmirnova were making their mark. When Théophile Gautier, the French poet and librettist of *Giselle*, visited St. Petersburg in 1858, he praised the Russian Ballet. 'There was no talk,' he wrote, 'no giggling or amorous glances at spectators or orchestra. This corps de ballet is carefully chosen from the Conservatoire. There are plenty of beauties, perfectly built, who know their profession – or their art, if you will – to perfection.'

The French influence persisted throughout the century and contributed greatly to the gracious style of the Russian dancers. Arthur St. Leon, who began his career as a violinist in the orchestra of the Paris Opera and then fell in love with ballet, mastered the classical technique and brought his gifts to St. Petersburg. He spent many years at the Maryinsky and among other ballets he produced *The Hump-Backed Horse*, the most Russian of Russian ballets. It is evident that the French masters, while contributing to the evolution of Russian classical dance, were able to integrate themselves into the Russian way of life and assimilate its indigenous music and its themes.

Finally yet another French ballet master, Marius Petipa, came to St. Petersburg in 1847 and remained there for the rest of his life, producing more than fifty ballets. He was the architect who guided the company to its greatest period, and with Lev Ivanov (one of the few Russian ballet masters during this period) he conceived the original *Swan Lake*. Yet more French influence and schooling came from the Swedish Christian Johannson, pupil of the pioneer of Danish ballet, August Bournonville, who came to the Imperial Theatre as a dancer and stayed to become the most revered ballet master in its entire history. But Johannson's French style was tempered with the Danish brilliance and élan of the Bournonville School, a fluent style with individual characteristics. It was he who refined and codified the classical style in all its purity and lyricism.

Not only did St. Petersburg possess the greatest repertoire of classical ballets and the finest company of dancers, but it was nourished by the leading native composers – Glinka, Glazounov, Balakirev, Arensky, the Russianized Viennese Ludwig Minkus, the Italian Roberto Drigo, and the greatest of all ballet composers, Tchaikovsky.

During the 1880s a remarkable personality shed her lustre

Marius Petipa.

upon St. Petersburg: Virginia Zucchi. Her sheer physical charm was a revelation that stimulated the Imperial Ballet anew. Zucchi brought the Italian merits of strong *pointes*, a bravura strength and impeccable balance. A dynamic performer with histrionic magnetism and a potent sexuality, she also had the gift of being unaffectedly natural. It was Zucchi who introduced the short tutu.

Her feminine allure endeared her to Russian audiences, and although there was great opposition to her entry into the Maryinsky, her supporters carried the day for a limited period. Zucchi was however criticized for her lack of style. She had not the easy-flowing grace of the French-Russian school, nor the finesse. Her influence did not assist the Russians in perfecting their school, but rather brought an emotional intensity and a sensuality of movement hitherto unknown in the aca-

Two portraits of Virginia Zucchi.

demic realm of prim and studied classicism. She brought a glow, a radiation.

It might be said that Zucchi enlarged the frontiers of ballet by her sensuality and dramatic power, which attracted a new and bigger audience, and it is certain that her exotic brilliance influenced the dancers and inspired them to greater expressiveness. Even the illustrious actor-manager Konstantine Stanislavsky was captivated by her. Zucchi loved to dance with the handsome Paul Gerdt, and she praised the Russian ballet of her day, but eventually even her great popularity with audiences could not prevent her dismissal from the Imperial stage through rival intrigues.

The splendour of this period was unparalleled, yet all was not blissful; there were shocks, there were undercurrents of artistic dissatisfaction and dissention. During the last years of the century the appearance of Enrico Cecchetti and the Italian ballerinas Carlotta Brianza and Pierina Legnani opened up a new phase that shook the old school to its foundations. Whereas the accent had been on grace, charm, artistry and personality, these visiting exponents of the Italian school brought strength, multiple *pirouettes*, flashing beats and speed. Their pyrotechnics made St. Petersburg audiences gasp with wonder.

Cecchetti was engaged by the Imperial Theatres as ballet master. For a while there were two separate schools operating within the Maryinsky – the Italian School of Cecchetti and the Franco-Danish-Russian School of Johannson. This division brought about a certain confusion and mixture of styles that has prevailed in Russian ballet ever since.

The ballet master Nicolai Legat was a devoted disciple of Christian Johannson. But he also appreciated the spectacular effects of the Italian technique, and was intrigued by Cecchetti and his methods. He learned and adopted some of its devices, and without forsaking the science and the exquisite style of Johannson, he grafted the technical expertize for turning *pirouettes* and beating *entrechats* onto the fluid grace of the Russian school. Before very long the Maryinsky ballerinas were as adept as the Italians.

Out of this era came the mightiest constellation of dancers the world has ever known. These brilliant stars of the Imperial Ballet included Anna Pavlova, Mathilde Kschesinska, Tamara Karsavina, Vera Trefilova, Lydia Kyasht, Olga Preobrajenska, Olga Spesivtzova, Vaslav Nijinsky, Mikhail Fokine, Adolf Bohm, Laurent Novikov and Anatole Obouk-

Christian Johannson.

Nicolai Legat.

15

Mikhail Fokine.

Anna Pavlova: a rare picture of the immortal ballerina who carried Russian ballet to the four corners of the earth.

Left, Vaslav Nijinsky, and Nijinsky with Tamara Karsavina in Spectre de la Rose.

hov, all of whom have contributed in large measure to the history of ballet.

Dancers have always been ahead of choreographers, but there were those who sought to rectify the lack of creators. Mikhail Fokine was one dancer turned choreographer who tried to break new ground. The visit to St. Petersburg of the American dancer Isadora Duncan in 1905 inspired him afresh, but the conservatism of the Court was hard to circumvent. At the head of the traditionalists was Nicolai Legat, aided and abetted by no less than the favourite dancer of the Tzar, Mathilde Kschesinska. The young Fokine fought to establish a wider expressive range, to allow the dancer to enter new fields. During this time of change ballet stood at the crossroads.

Fokine found an ally in Serge Diaghilev, the inscrutable connoisseur who first made a name by publishing *Mir Isskustvo*, a revolutionary magazine of the arts. Diaghilev failed to gain a footing in the Imperial Theatres, but stayed on the fringe, and saw a future in exporting Russian art to the West. Once nicknamed 'the silver beaver' because of a white streak of hair on his forehead, he was the supreme opportunist.

During the first decade of the twentieth century, the ballet of St. Petersburg blossomed into a renaissance with the glory of its dancers. When Diaghilev brought the Imperial Ballet to Paris in 1909, and the following year to London, the impact

Marina Zest rehearsing with Kulichev-skaya, accompanied by the famous violinist Isaye, 1911.

Male corps de ballet in class, 1911.

Mathilde Kschesinskaya (Princess Romanovsky-Kschesinsky), favourite dancer of Tzar Nicholas II.

Serge Diaghilev with his secretary-collaborator, Boris Kochno.

was sensational: every strata of artistic life was stunned and stimulated by the exoticism and the grandeur of those consummate artists. Indeed, the repercussions have continued right up to the present time, and there are still a few privileged ones who live to tell of the wonder.

At the height of this golden epoch of ballet came the war of 1914, and afterwards the Bolshevik Revolution of 1917. St. Petersburg became Petrograd, a city in travail, and for a time the very existence of the ballet was threatened. During the period of the troubles many dancers fled abroad to try to pursue their art. Others stayed and grappled with the fearsome problems of survival. Diaghilev remained abroad and became the repository of emigré Russian talent; but though he was a skilled manipulator and impresario, he was more knowledgeable about painting and music than about the dance itself. During the twenty-odd years of his Ballet Russe's existence in the West, the flow of talent from St. Petersburg-Petrograd-Leningrad dried up; the first impact withered, the originals faded away, and to fill the gap the arch-sorcerer exploited novelty, innovation, shock and finally absurdity, to take the place of the sensuous and magical essence of glorious dance that had been the substance of the original enchantment.

With his blend of snobbery, ultra-sophistication and decadence, Diaghilev was the key figure who sign-posted the way of art in the West, and indicated the path of fashion in almost every walk of life. While in Russia the purity, spirituality and sincerity of the art continued, and despite many hazards, setbacks and calamities the school progressed within the same pattern, Diaghilev during his nomadic wanderings failed to establish a sound, all-embracing school, and the quality of dance became dissipated and secondary to the trappings and eccentricities of the new balletic image.

Meanwhile in Petrograd some revolutionaries wanted to close down the Imperial Theatres, which they considered to be the extravagant and frivolous luxuries of the Court and aristocracy, but in his wisdom Lenin and his first commissar of the arts, Anatole Lunacharsky, saved the day for ballet and the arts in Soviet Russia by establishing the Imperial Theatres as Academic Theatres, endowing them and their attendant schools, thus ensuring that these national institutions continued to function in the same tradition for the cultural needs and the social benefit of the people.

Thus the tradition of the Maryinsky continued without a break through those turbulent times. The theatre was renamed

Kirov after one of the heroes of the Revolution, Sergei Mironovitch Kirov, a member of the Politburo and First Secretary of the Leningrad District Council, who was later to be assassinated in Smolny on 1st December, 1934. The school became the Leningrad Choreographic Academy, later to be renamed after Agrippina Vaganova, under whose guidance the school of Petipa, Johannson, Gerdt, Sokolova and Legat was carried on. Her fellow teachers included Romanov, Vecheslova-Snetkova, Shiraev, Ponomarev, Lopukov and Bochorov.

The 'twenties saw the building up of Leningrad's school of dance, bringing an abundance of qualities – ecstatic lyricism, heroic virility, plastic sensuousness of powerful dimensions. From Vaganova's enthusiasm and inspired leadership came a new flowering of ballerinas with exceptional gifts: Marina Semenova, Olga Jordan, Tamara Vecheslova, Natalia Dudins-

Olga Spesivtseva

Agrippina Vaganova.

kaya, Galina Kirilova and Alla Shelest. Equally remarkable was the new line of male dancers whose dominating power and stature generated a magnetism and a mystique that lifted the dance to new heights. Such phenomenal artists as Alexei Yermoleyev, Vahktung Chabukiani, Konstantine Sergeyev, and many others brought to fruition the noble style of the Soviet Ballet.

About this time the theatre of drama was particularly active in throwing off the shackles of convention and in reflecting new moods and images. With powerful emphasis it brought new trends and techniques of play production. In the conflict of ideas many theories were tried out: realism, symbolism, futurism, constructivism were just some of the slogans that heralded a movement towards more expressive theatre. The creators of ballet saw these experiments and took note. They too felt the necessity to break new ground, to explore.

The surge of innovation and choreographic development which had begun before the Revolution was now taken up by such giants as Rotislav Zakharov, Vasily Vainonen, Fedor Lopukov, Vakhtang Chabukiani and Leonid Lavrovsky. These men enlarged the histrionic as well as the choreographic range of the ballet spectacle; they welcomed new devices and made use of the advancing technical skills, speed, momentum, acrobatics, geometric and irregular patterns, spacial lifts, and everything that contributed to a fuller expression of dance.

Thus the art of choreography developed from the romantic, the abstract, from fairy tales to human and down-to-earth

Left, Vaslav Nijinsky; centre, Elena Liukum as Tao Hoa in The Red Poppy; *below, Boris Shavrov in* The Red Poppy.

realities. Dance embraced social and political themes. The formal epic ballet appeared, inspired by the new Soviet realism. Many of these ballets – for instance, *The Red Poppy, The Bronze Horseman, Jeanne d'Arc* – are seldom performed. They were of their time; and time brings alterations in conditions and changes in taste and fashions.

The new creators and artists gave to the Leningrad Ballet the essence of the Russian character and the Russian soul. The old-fashioned traditional mime gestures gave way to a more expressive dance and more realistic acting. The innate lyricism remained, but was stretched to a more florid and sweeping movement. The heroic ballet broke upon the scene, introducing a symphonic style. The male dancer was elevated to equal status with the ballerina; great aerial movements and acrobatic lifts brought new dimensions; and all this new brilliance, this vital surge of exuberance grew logically out of the old foundations of this long continuing school.

Leonid Lavrovsky.

Such composers as Asafiev, Kachaturian, Glière, Krein, Prokofiev and Shostakovich composed the new music, and the choreographers went to work with a consuming passion. Rotislav Zakharov with his production of *The Fountain of Bakhchiserai,* Leonid Lavrovsky with his masterly interpretation of *Giselle* and his monumental *Romeo and Juliet,* Vasily Vainonen with his stirring *Flames of Paris* and his charmingly gentle *Nutcracker,* and Fedor Lopukov with his new acrobatic innovations in *Ice Maiden* and *Dance Symphony,* ensured an era of exciting development.

During this auspicious period there came from the school and from the hand of Vaganova a young dancer of genius who was destined to rise to great heights, a deeply sensitive artist with a perceptive mentality, a kind of inborn wisdom, and a poet's heart. Galina Ulanova's soul shone through everything she did. The master-choreographers Zakharov and Lavrovsky were inspired by her ability to live her rôles and project infinite shades of human feeling. Audiences were hypnotized by the poignancy and truth of her portrayals. Her total absorption in every aspect of a rôle made them feel that they were in a sacred presence. Such a rare and consummate artist had never been seen before, and indeed may never be seen again.

Further mention must be made here of the choreographic genius and brilliant stagecraft of Leonid Lavrovsky. Before attempting to stage such a dramatic work as *Romeo and Juliet,* Lavrovsky sought advice and help from the eminent theatre

Vakhtang Chaboukiani as Othello.

Galina Ulanova, an early portrait.

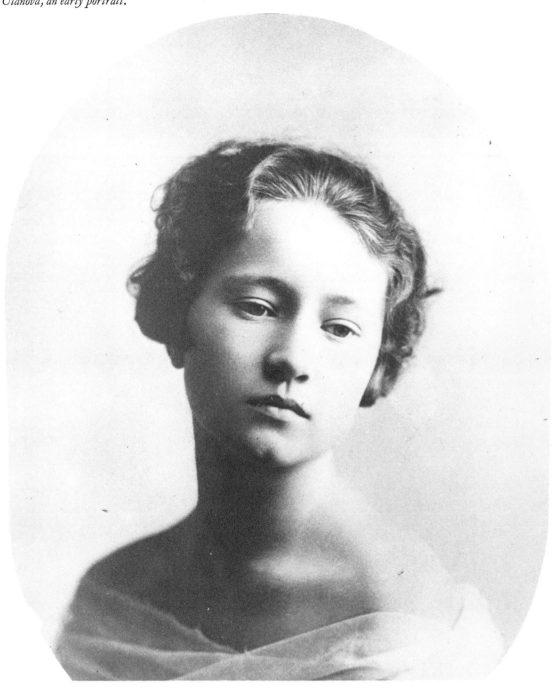

*Opposite, the restless temperament of
Galina Ulanova in childhood is recorded
by these scribbles on her school locker:
'Two days before the end of studies.'
'Four days to Graduation performance.'
'One month before finishing school.
Hurrah! Hurrah!! Ulanova, 12th
May.'*

director and producer of Shakespeare, Sergei Radlov. With the help of leading producers from the drama theatre, Lavrovsky succeeded in expanding the histrionic content of ballet. His *Romeo and Juliet* broke new ground, giving proof that the dance can express the poetry and the narrative of Shakespeare's play as eloquently as the spoken word. This ballet took years to produce and has become the prototype for many imitators; but none, despite much plagiarism, succeeded in producing anything comparable in immensity, grandeur, poignancy or style.

During the Second World War the arts were again in peril. The long siege of Leningrad necessitated the Kirov Ballet's evacuation to Perm, but it never stopped producing and performing ballet for the troops and the workers. In Perm it continued to cultivate its school and prepare young dancers for the future. Again the long unbroken tradition survived and the beauty of its dance was undiminished. After the war the Kirov Ballet returned to Leningrad and renewed itself in the beautiful city which, despite its sufferings, remains the most serene of northern cities.

The war inspired yet another era of such heroic and tragic ballets as the *Leningrad Symphony* and revivals of *Spartacus*. After the war, the phase of choreographic development continued with vital and adventurous works from Leonid Jacobson, Igor Belsky, Yuri Grigorovitch and Konstantine Sergeyev, who found mellifluous accompaniment and rich thematic textures in the symphonic works of Russia's leading composers, Prokofiev, Shostakovitch and Katchaturian.

In recent years these choreographers have developed and matured, bringing forth a steady stream of notable ballets. Outstanding perhaps is Konstantine Sergeyev's *Hamlet*, a skilful adaptation of Shakespeare's masterpiece. With astringent economy of means and a cogent style of dance mime – and despite drastic cuts and omissions – he succeeded in sketching a taut drama in a genre that brings the histrionic power of classical dance closer to articulate eloquence. With the modern dissonances of Tchervinsky's tension-laden music, Sergeyev carried the narrative dance drama a step farther. It is remarkable that Leningrad's choreographers have proved so adept at interpreting Shakespeare.

For the past decade and longer, Konstantine Sergeyev was artistic director and principal ballet master at the Kirov. He is now artistic director of the Vaganova Choreographic Academy. His wife, Natalia Dudinskaya, has been leader, teacher and répétiteur to the school and company. Madame Dudinskaya was trained by Vaganova, and has many memories. A superb dancer of fire and passion with a formidable technique, she was acclaimed and adored by all who saw her in her heyday. In her head she carries the nuances and refinements of the great classical repertoire. She has helped to produce yet another line of ballerinas whose superlative qualities have dazzled the world, and roused even the sternest critics to ecstasy.

Such dancers as Irina Kolpakova, Alla Sizova, Gabriella

Caricature of Agrippina Vaganova by Nicolai Legat.

Left, Vaganova at rehearsal; below, her last graduating class, with Irina Kolpakova leading.

Vaganova taking a class with, from left: Alla Osipenko (second), Ludmilla Komiserova (fourth), Irina Kolpakova (sixth).

Komleva, Alla Osipenko, Olga Moiseyeva are of the highest order; yet they do not outshine the men, for there are male classical and character dancers whose magnificent virtuosity is breathtaking. Sergei Vikulov, Vladilen Semenov, Alexander Pavlovsky, Vadim Budharin, Konstantine Rassadin, Gennady Selyutsky, among so many more, are dancers who bring power, excitement and physical ecstasy to ballet.

One never-to-be-forgotten occasion occurred at Covent Garden during the 1961 London season of the Kirov Ballet when *Taras Bulba* was given with an all-male cast. The men of the Kirov excelled themselves, performing Fenster's vigorous choreography with fantastic aplomb. Like wild Cossack horsemen they leapt and whirled, defying the laws of gravity, and reached such a frenzy yet with such controlled panache, that their accelerations and explosions of energy sent the audience into a state of hysteria. When the curtain came down the applause was wild and deafening. One feared for the walls of the ancient Opera House. The applause continued long after the orchestra had gone home and the lights were lowered. Again and again the curtain was raised, and still the applause went on undiminished. Only the lowering of the iron safety curtain finally brought the evening to a close.

This was a unique event when the male dancers of the Kirov momentarily eclipsed the matchless excellence of its ballerinas, but perhaps only because the ballerinas were absent from the scene. These wonderful dancers delight audiences and evoke tumultuous applause by the brilliance and ease of their physical exploits in the classical genre and in their own folk idiom, whenever and wherever they appear. Nevertheless, these

Rudolf Nureyev.

Natalia Makarova.

Mikhail Baryshnikov.

appearances outside their own frontiers have led to some disturbing repercussions.

In St. Petersburg days the Court Theatres guarded their dancers jealously; only the very privileged stars such as Pavlova, Kschesinska, Trefilova, Karsavina and their male partners were permitted to undertake commercial engagements abroad, and then only for short periods. Today, in changed circumstances, the situation has some similarities. The Soviet government also guards its dancers most zealously, and although the Kirov and Bolshoi Ballets make regular tours abroad, their dancers are not permitted to accept long-term or permanent engagements in foreign countries. Inevitably the Kirov's tours abroad have sometimes opened the eyes of dancers to the horizons that lie beyond the boundaries of their motherland, and some artists have been tempted to break away from the country and the system that nurtured them.

It is a sad thought that these dancers are no longer mentioned in the annals of Soviet Ballet. They are considered by their own people to be deserters, disloyal and dishonest, who without leave or permission renounced their citizenship and broke their contract with the company that schooled them and gave them the opportunity to become artists. Great art demands great loyalty. The loyalty of the Kirov dancers is inspired by love of their art, love of their country and their city, and an overriding pride in the historic family to which they belong. This is why when one of the family defects there is consternation and bitterness at home. Looking at the situation in a patriotic light one might accept as justifiable the condemnation of those whose trust has been betrayed. Yet if officialdom could take a more lenient view of the instability and frailty of genius, such artists as Rudolf Nureyev, Natalia Makarova, and Mikhail Baryshnikov might be considered the most eloquent ambassadors of Leningrad's Ballet. Certainly the phenomenon of the Kirov dancers has extended a remarkable influence over the growth and style of ballet in every part of the world. It has awakened and stimulated the love of ballet in people in every walk of life, but even more than this it has influenced and uplifted the quality of dance. Eventually, perhaps, the Soviet government will find itself able to take pride in the achievements of such dancers and acknowledge their importance in the history of Russian Ballet.

So often Leningrad has sacrificed its greatest treasures to benefit the progress of other companies. What heart-break it must have been to lose Ulanova to the Bolshoi . . . to lose

Nureyev and another student with their teacher, Alexander Pushkin.

Baryshnikov as Vestri, God of the Dance, choreographed by Leonid Jacobsen.

Lavrovsky and Grigorovich to the Bolshoi ... One could make a long list of Leningrad's contributions and losses, but fortunately the fountain of Leningrad's genius is never-ending, never in danger of drying up.

Today on the Kirov stage there are yet more exquisite new ballerinas: the adorable Svetlana Efremova, the sublime Elena Evteyeva, the joyous Valentina Hannibalova, the impeccable Lubov Konakova, the invincible Olga Chenchikova ... and with them are the new male dancers: Kovmir, Gulyayev, Breznoi, Blankov – they come again and again, like the tides of the sea.

'The artist must love life and have the ability to observe it. . . . To see in it all that is bright and beautiful, all that is necessary to one's work.'

GALINA ULANOVA

Dancers of the future in a school performance.

The Life of the School

The story of the Leningrad Ballet is a perpetual fairy-tale, an enduring fable in which the Good Fairy always triumphs. In the previous chapter glimpses of its history revealed a continuing ascendancy throughout the tumult of living experience. There are reasons for its enduring progress, and perhaps one of these is that Russians are born dancers. Dancing is in their blood; their temperament and spirit give all; limitations of physical power are transcended, and nothing is held back. When singleness of purpose is taken up and nurtured, and when the finest ballet masters of Europe are gathered to cultivate the art, the result can scarcely be less than exceptional.

This chapter looks at the Leningrad Ballet of today. We shall go in winter and in summer and savour Leningrad and its dancers. We shall visit the Kirov Theatre, entering from the cold and gloomy streets into the elegance of its baroque splendours – its marble, its chandeliers – and we shall see the classics in their most sublime form. But first to the school, the hub of creation, to see how such an institution works, how it unravels the creative process, how it conjures and presents dancers of supreme eloquence.

The Agrippina Vaganova Choreographic Academy in Rossi Street is the same Leningrad Kirov Academic school, the same Imperial school of older times, which for 240 years has produced all the great dancers in classical ballet. The school and the old building have remained inseparable over the years. The changes brought about by time have been effected with a quiet, smiling grace, as though changes were all for the better. Changes in the physical nature of the building are almost as unnoticeable as those in the unfolding tradition of dance. Generations of pupils have worn out countless pairs of shoes on these smooth floors, ballets have been rehearsed here ad infinitum, the polishing process continues to give an even higher gloss, the same creative evolution is manifest afresh, and the pride and joy in the work is undiminished.

The stout old building stands secure, its raked studios intact; its vaulted windows, its iron balustrades, its antiquated elevator, all speak of history! At the very heart of it is its intimate museum, a shabby room crammed with relics of illustrious ballerinas, their shoes, their wigs, their jewelry, their costumes – faded, shrivelled, yet poignant in their reminder of youthful blood. Here, too, are albums and tattered fragments of programmes, chronicles of fame. The dusty silence of the room of excitements past, waiting to be reborn . . .

The labyrinthine corridors of this old mill of tortuous labours seem to hold a nostalgic enchantment that is like a heady perfume. One is lost amidst the rambling floors encrusted with studios and tiny practice rooms; so many inlets, so many doors and corners, a veritable warren. It is a silent building yet alive with whispers, echoing with the hushed voices of children and the half-drowned music of classes. In its corridors a little bevy of fair-haired girls presses forward to curtsey. These demoiselles in black and white and wearing red neckerchiefs appear on every landing and at every corner to welcome visitors with unaffected graciousness.

First day of term.

32

Flowers for the teachers.

Do they feel the hallowed presences – where the aging Johannson strutted with his turned-out feet, where Legat tuned his fiddle, where Fokine fretted when Petipa reigned supreme, where Pavel Gerdt extolled charm, where Nijinsky first felt the rapture of his feline talent, where Kschesinska played courtesan, and Pavlova rose to grace, where Karsavina first captivated the critics? Are these exuberant children aware of the ghosts of the mighty who walk these corridors?

Pupils come from all over the world to receive the blessings of the Leningrad School, as well as from the many regions within the Soviet hemisphere – Slav, Georgian, Khirgiz, Moldavian, Ukrainian. All are hopeful that exposure to the inspiration of this place will mould their talent to perfection, and impart the hallmarks of grace and style. The boys are less numerous than the girls, but equally impressive. They pass in ones and twos – sleek, long-haired, with sensitive brows and serious eyes, boys who have taken to dance as naturally as Western boys take to football or baseball. These boys relish their classes; but they live for performances when they don

Sculpture by Peter Carlovitch Klodt on the Anitchkov bridge.

Kazan Cathedral, Nevsky Prospect.

Across the frozen Neva – St. Peter and Paul Fortress.

the uniforms of Suvorovtsy cadets (named after the famous General Suvorov) and dance quadrilles with the girls.

For the most part dance is taught in segregated classes, so that concentration may be entirely on essentials. In some young groups and also in selective lessons there are mixed classes. Later of course, boy meets girl in the *pas de deux* class and in rehearsals, but there is no atmosphere of segregation, for boys and girls roam freely in the school, meeting in corridors, in the canteen, forming friendships, exchanging experiences and discussing the future of ballet. It is all as natural as any well-organized community should be.

How different, one imagines, from the days when Anna Pavlova was a child, when little girls were kept apart from little boys, and there was no distraction and no incentive but dance and practice. 'In my time,' Karsavina said, 'we did ballet in the morning, and ballet in the afternoon. In the evenings when our time was free, we chose ballet again. The windows of the studio were too high to see the outside world, so there was nothing else to do but practise our ballet, and this we grew to love.'

But the hard discipline of the daily class is sweetened by numerous rehearsals which presage performances. The Suvorovtsy cadets, the waltzes, the quadrilles, the mazurkas, the abundant Nutcrackers and many other pieces make up the repertoire for end-of-term displays and graduation performances that bring thrills and excitements to break up the repetition of the daily routine. But more than this, there are occasions when the young ones perform on the Kirov stage in *The Nutcracker, The Sleeping Beauty, Cinderella, Don Quixote* and other works.

The children are an integral part of the Kirov ensemble, as are the old and retired dancers who remain with the company as part of the *mise-en-scène* – one great family in art to interpret the full score from youth to age.

The foundations of family life are firmly rooted in this large ensemble, rendering it more human and seemingly closer to normal life. Families predominate – *babushkas* (grandmothers) are part of the *ménage*. Side by side with the splendours of the stage go little incidents of human drama – manifestations of individual affection and personal conflict, comradely admiration and competitive rivalry, feuds and factions . . . all contained within the bounds of etiquette and convention. Generations of children and dancers' children – and are not all dancers forever children? – follow in the tradition of their forebears, united by a vocation to which many of them are born.

For days and weeks and months the powdery snow falls upon Leningrad, bringing silence and beauty. Sometimes a leaden greyness settles over the old city, so majestic and remote, imposing a gloom, a colourless melancholy. The hard winter seems to be a challenge to movement: the swirl of the Neva is arrested by slabs of ice, the very stillness is held in an icy grip. Within this frozen dreamland of enchantment the ballet school is a reality, a ruthless institution of artistic purpose in which the hearts and minds of the children are strengthened with steel-like resolve. Yet there is something still of the grace and charm of the Court in the conduct of the school, something of the world of play-acting and children's games, an illusion which must be treasured, for thus are these tender *malchiki* (young children) kept pure and lively, and tinged with a glow from the old fire.

From the rhythmic tread, day after day, on those old wooden floors worn smooth by the splashing of water from a can and by the sliding, skimming, pushing, jumping feet of legions of children, from the agility of these boys forever as spirited as the prancing horses on the Anichkov Bridge, from the quiet zeal of these girls, so modest and gentle, comes an ever-renewed joy in the work.

Not all is ballet ... Lessons must be learned.

To be chosen for this school is almost like receiving a divine accolade! To enter upon a career in ballet entails a kind of renunciation, like entering the Church. After acceptance, the child enters a world in which submission is total. Out of that submission grows a new backbone, source of strength, agility and stamina. The individual ego is not crushed or damaged; it emerges during the training period. The skill of each particular student asserts itself according to the innate talent and the acquisition of knowledge, together with inspirational stimulus and the prodding of ambition.

When one pupil falls by the wayside, there are twenty more ready to fall in . . .

The organization of the school and company is scarcely perceptible even to the regular observer – like the tip of an iceberg. There is no computer-like slickness here, no streamlined efficiency, no obvious rigid order; instead an old-world muddle, charm and commotion pervades. The architecture within is the result of adaptation and change, a making-do with what is available and only what is essential. Nevertheless, the school is an interlocking organization that has the ramifications of a vast empire. From the plain, homespun, everyday ordinariness of routine, miracles are achieved.

Music is an essential part of the young dancer's education.
Male students practise duets.

It is all managed by adherence to tradition, and while this tradition is followed with meticulous care, there can be no danger of breakdown or failure. Logistics have been well digested, and forward planning takes care of every eventuality – the machine rolls on regardless. The annual intake of pupils is limited to 100 children. Biological statistics are considered by the Selection Committee. The physical tests are simple but all-embracing. The results of this Committee's deliberations are joy and heart-break. The quest is talent and the mission, development of that talent. Decisions are based upon the evaluation of potential rather than upon pedigree.

Starting at the age of nine the children enter for an 8 year course. Some older children are taken at the age of thirteen for what is known as an Experimental 6-year Course. It is said that children who enrol in this course sometimes progress more rapidly because their application stems from a more mature intellect. A small proportion of exceptionally gifted students are admitted for a 2- to 3-year course. Thus there are openings for the very talented at three different stages of development.

The average working complement of the school is estimated at between 450 and 480 pupils, taught by some 76 specialist teachers. The categories of the teachers may be listed thus:

Classical Ballet	42	Historical dance	7
Pas de deux	5	Acting skills	4
Character-Ethnic	17	Fencing	1

Teacher and students listen informally to a fellow student.

Opposite, the gymnasium assists in developing masculine strength and fencing aids poise and agility.

There are 18 music teachers, mainly professors of the piano; 26 concert masters – musical coaches; 33 teachers of general education, which includes languages, history, geography, science, mathematics and gymnastics. The social sciences are not neglected, so that those children who do not make the grade as dancers will be equipped for the necessities of life. There are recreational clubs, and for those who at an early age seek to reach out beyond the confines of the ballet, to learn something of how their country is governed, there is the Young Pioneers Corps.

More than half of the total complement of the school – some 210 children – are housed nearby in the school hostel. Of these about 40 are foreigners. The rest are day pupils living at home, or with relatives. That is the set-up and capacity of this unique school. During recent times many ballet schools throughout the world have been organized on a similar pattern, but without, as yet, any comparable results.

The Vaganova Choreographic Academy has close connections with the Conservatoire, which is housed in a large building opposite the Kirov theatre. The Conservatoire is mainly concerned with the training of opera singers, but there

Students cleaning the canteen windows – menial tasks are also part of the routine.

is a ballet department specializing in the teaching of choreography and production. Pietr Gusev, the venerable director, is a noted choreographer and producer of the classics. The Vaganova Academy, whose most recent director is Janina Lushina, gives regular school performances on the Conservatoire stage, and it is here that parents may watch the progress of their children.

The most daunting aspect of the ballet as a profession is the large percentage of waste; but perhaps waste is the wrong word. No effort that is spent in ballet training is wasted, even if the recipient of that training does not make the grade. The training and discipline equips the pupil to make good in other spheres. But one cannot ignore that there are many heartaches. Ballet is a world in which ruthless driving power is subject to chance and hazard, of which physical development is not the least; thus, out of a total of more than 280 girls and 170 boys, the number of pupils graduating in one year is approximately 44 Russian and 5 foreign girls; 14 Russian and 2 foreign boys. From this small out-put of first-class talent the Kirov Ballet takes but 3 to 5 girls, and from 1 to 3 boys in a year. Other graduates find places in the Maly theatre ballet, a second

A group of young pioneers.

Young students performing the Nut-cracker pas de trois on the stage of the Philharmonic Hall.

Opposite, children dancing the Nut-cracker pas de trois.

company with slightly lower standards. Some are taken into the Leonide Jacobson touring company, and others find work in modern dance companies, and in provincial companies or in Variety, skating shows and films. Some teach, and others find their way into other professions.

Statistics can make desolate reading, and like all cold analysis they are sometimes alien to actual conditions. These figures seem unrealistic when compared with the manifold resources of the Kirov with its battalions of dancers, its teachers, répétiteurs, choreographers and producers. Its tremendous range of artists, its duplicate casts, its great corps de ballet, are made up of many vintages of dancers, from the fledgling graduate to the veteran on the threshold of retirement.

One can see a dovetailing through the whole passage of ballet creation, from youth to age, from apprentice to mature artist; this integral interlocking extends to every department; from conception to blue-print, from rehearsal to performance; it extends even to the apportioning of time and space. Space is utilized with the utmost economy. Many studios occupied

with student classes from 8.30 in the morning are taken over by the theatre company later in the day for classes and rehearsals. Thus a pupil of the school remains a pupil throughout his or her career, even after graduating to the Kirov.

The old buildings in Rossi Street, so dilapidated and creaking with age behind the noble façade, have recently been undergoing repair. For a time the front door was blocked by builder's trestles, bags of cement and such like. One had to enter from the rear of the building, finding one's way through numerous doors and winding stairs, to reach eventually the lobby and cloakrooms, where the aging lady commissioner always sits with the inevitable glass of lemon tea and a timeless patience, through summer and winter. Her whispered conversations with pupils, teachers and visitors are always a source of intriguing curiosity. Her kindly welcome to the Cradle of Ballet never loses its freshness, and never fails to send a tingle down the spine. One prays that automation and new-fangled technology will never be allowed in this door. Long may everything remain as it is!

A great favourite with performers and audiences is the Suvorovtsy Quadrille, named after the famous General Suvorov.

Opposite above, the Examination Commission.

Opposite below, examination class — the Pillow Dance from Lavrovsky's Romeo and Juliet.

Right, a prayer before the exam.

Below, Graduation Day for Irina Tchisyakova.

Natalia Dudinskaya and Konstantine Sergeyev demonstrating the Polonaise.

The School as part of My Life

KONSTANTINE SERGEYEV

I developed an interest in ballet when it was already too late to enter a ballet school. I was fourteen. Sitting at my desk during some class of arithmetic, physics or chemistry, in my imagination I was far away, living in the miraculous world of Swan Lake. I never missed a single performance at the former Maryinsky theatre, and from high up in the gallery I admired the magic art of ballet which I judged to be quite unattainable. Among the subjects forming our school curriculum I preferred athletics. In our spacious gymnasium, like the legendary Icarus, I craved to fly.

Fortunately for me, in the year 1924 the Leningrad Ballet School opened evening classes for beginners which older girls and boys were allowed to join, and suddenly there I was at No. 2, Rossi Street (formerly Theatre Street), standing at the barre and doing the first ballet steps.

Sergeyev gives the boys' class.

After four years of practice I acquired enough proficiency to enable me to join a touring ballet company headed by a well-known character dancer, Joseph Kschesinsky – brother of Mathilde Kschesinska. I was lured there by my idée fixe -- the possibility of dancing principal parts in the various ballets, but especially that of Prince Siegfried in Swan Lake. After covering thousands of kilometres by railroad across the Urals, Siberia and the Far East, I still did not forsake my wish to complete my dance education. Returning to Leningrad I succeeded in passing the required examinations and was admitted to the graduation class of the School of Choreography.

The following year the doors of the Kirov Theatre of Opera and Ballet were wide open to me, and ever since that time ballet has been my life, and the Ballet School at No. 2, Rossi Street my second home. It was there that all the classes and rehearsals of the Kirov company took place; it was there that I perfected my dancing skill; it was there that I took my first steps as a teacher; it was there that I embarked upon my career of choreographer.

For full thirty-five years I danced the entire classical and contemporary repertoire, inheriting from my teachers my favourite rôles of Prince Siegfried and of Count Albrecht. As actor-dancer I had the good fortune to be the first interpreter of the part of Romeo opposite Gálina Ulanova's Juliet in the Prokofiev-Lavrovsky production of Romeo and Juliet. The depth of feelings experienced by the characters created by Shakespeare has never ceased to impress my fancy. Moreover, in my own endeavours I have felt a constant attraction to unravel complicated psychological rôles. This eventually found an outlet in my choreographic work.

My first major creation was the ballet Cinderella to the music of Sergei Prokofiev, in which I also danced the part of the Prince. In my collaboration with Prokofiev I aimed at extending forms of classical ballet. The next difficult task to fall to my lot was the composition of new versions of classical ballets such as Raymonda, The Sleeping Beauty, Le Corsaire, and Swan Lake. In 1971 I choreographed Hamlet to a score by the Leningrad composer, N. Tchervinsky. Previously I created The Path of Thunder to music by Kara-Karayev – a story of a white girl and a coloured youth cruelly murdered because 'their only fault was to love each other'.

More recently it was with great enthusiasm that I composed a ballet, or rather a public spectacle, to a score by B. Alexandrov, about a talented Russian craftsman, a patriot of his native country, nicknamed Levsha [Lefthander], a character who managed to shoe an outlandish curiosity – a steel flea!

For fourteen years I directed the Kirov company, handing down my experience of the Russian school of classical dance to the younger

Sergeyev rehearses Swan Lake.

generation of dancers who glorified the Leningrad Kirov Ballet both at home and on its travels throughout the world. Apart from my activities as choreographer at the Kirov Theatre I continue to be closely connected with No. 2, Rossi Street in my capacity as artistic director and choreographer of the Leningrad School of Choreography, named after Agrippina Vaganova.

My recent production of Alexander Glazounov's ballet The Four Seasons, *casting students of different grades – from the youngest children to graduating students, proved to be a useful stage practice for the new generation. The story of the ballet is full of meaning – the four seasons signify the evolution of life, the coming and going of succeeding generations . . .*

I take a joy and pride in my work.'

Natalia Dudinskaya—always a joy in her work.

My Philosophy is Dance

NATALIA DUDINSKAYA

Since my earliest recollections ballet has been my life. My mother, Natalia Dudinskaya-Tagliori, was a dancer. She had a large private school in Kharkov. At the age of seven I commenced my first steps under her guidance, and she taught me to love dance and music. In brief it was she who initiated me into the wonderful world of art.

When I was ten my mother took me to Leningrad where I entered the Leningrad Ballet School. When I reached the advanced stage of the school curriculum I was fortunate to be selected for the class of our great teacher, Professor Agrippina Vaganova. In the year 1931 I left the Ballet School and joined the Kirov Company.

In my professional career there are two persons to whom I am infinitely grateful and to whom I owe everything that I have achieved — they are my mother and Agrippina Vaganova. I had the rare distinction of working under Professor Vaganova for twenty-three years;

Dudinskaya discussing her class with the author and his wife.

*three years at the Ballet School, and twenty years in her class of per-
fection for the soloists of the Kirov Company. Oh, the happiness it
gave me!*

*A ballet class is planned anew every day on the basis of the previous
one. There is always something spontaneous and new in our classes
despite the working-out and re-working of previous material. In this
process the teacher creates something new based on tradition; hence
the method evolves, it moves forward.*

*In my classes I try to preserve carefully the foundations of Vaga-
nova's method, which enables the dancer to conquer fully her body. It
is not only the legs and the arms of the dancer, but also her torso,
shoulders, neck and head that must be expressive.*

*The art of ballet is not a museum. The demands of changing times
are always reflected in art. Ballet technique has greatly progressed and
continues to advance. It requires virtuoso sequences, new movements,
jumps and rotations to be introduced into the class. Everything is
changing and moving forward. Teachers of classical dance cannot and
must not stand still. We, the pupils of the great Vaganova, must
develop her method and perfect the foundations inherited from her*

Dudinskaya rehearsing the cygnets.

Dudinskaya coaching Vorontzeva.

still further. Inevitably present-day classes – and among them my own – differ in some measure from those of my teacher, though I hold her precepts sacred.

It would be an interesting study to follow the evolution in teaching classical dance, for instance to compare the classes of Christian Johannson with those of his pupil Nicolai Legat, and again Legat's classes with those of his pupil Agrippina Vaganova and so on . . .

For my part, it seems to me that most of all I like to work with the young and the aspiring. They give me the greatest satisfaction. But I feel equally at home in the class-room and in the theatre. Our numerous dancers and I consider the task of perfecting technique to be interminable. We are happy when we are improving details because they result in improving the whole. Time and experience lead to still greater perfection. I think that ballet science is a kind of philosophy. I do not want, and I cannot imagine, any other life where I might be as much absorbed in my work and have such close contact with my surroundings.'

'Only by love and hard work can you become a good dancer . . . love of hard work and love of the art. Dancing is no art for the faint-hearted. Not a few there were, even in Russia, who, having put their hands to the plough, turned back. The school and the theatre were well rid of them. The sieve had a wide mesh. Only the great remained.'

NICOLAI LEGAT

The Class

The Class is the structure that forms the dancer; a science devised in continuity by generations of ballet masters, built upon the simple formula of relaxation and tension. It creates the human instrument for the expression of emotions in movement. It develops the dancer's personality, line and style; it guides his talent to accomplishment, and keeps him tuned to the pursuit of perfection.

In the beginning there is the test; simple credentials; a genetic history that is compatible, a supple physique, a musical sensibility and the gift of memory – these are essentials.

Learning such an art as ballet is a mystical process in which the heart and mind of the pupil are influenced, not only by the indoctrination and process of training, or the love of a particular teacher, but by innate talent and spiritual fervour.

Recently the early years of ballet training have been codified and documented in precise terms: the daily routine is slow and careful, and almost severe in the sparsity of dance movement that is permitted. The training is geared to a gentle, gradual – one might say, natural – development which, with the unfolding of time and the growth of the pupil, cultivates an aura of simple eloquence. The disciplines and dynamic tensions the body is subjected to are never brutal. The dancers grow up without strain; they learn to wear their technical prowess as comfortably and unobtrusively as a favourite well-worn garment.

Fundamentally there is always joy in the work, an abundant freshness that lends exuberance to routine, makes every lesson special and pleasing. Every class is different, yet each class contains a unity of approach and application. Refinement and beauty are fashioned from toughened sinews; strength is developed that attains to the superhuman. Only by exceptional effort may exceptional results be obtained.

What are the secrets of technique that distinguish this School? They lie in the particular use of the traditional exercises devised by the old masters – a balance between tension and relaxation used in every variety of rhythm, and developing from small to large and powerful movements. The code reads thus:

First, the **Stance** – the position which gives the body access to movement. In the perfect stance the back is the centre of control. The solar plexus is the centre of feeling – all movement comes from the centre out, and comes with the co-ordination of all the contributing parts of the body; the shoulders held down, the arms rounded, the ribs flat, the buttocks tucked under to enable the complete (unnatural) turn-out of the legs from hip to ankle; the neck uplifted supporting a proud head.

Second, the **Grands pliés** – the smooth action of a spring – the mainspring of action, slow and controlled, warming the whole body to participation.

Third, the **Battements tendus** in multiple rhythms – repetitive stretching and relaxing of the foot, developing an instep of steel and rounded beauty.

Fourth, the **Battements jetés** that bring lightness, speed and dexterity to the movements of the legs.

Fifth, the **Battements fondus**, the deep fondu (*demi-plié*) bringing strength that cultivates a melting softness – *ballon* – the facility to alight effortlessly from flight.

Opposite, the child's physical potential is examined.

The Selection Committee.

Sixth, the **Battements frappés**, the dynamic throw of the leg from relax to stretch – the strengthening of the vital knee joint. Incorporated with *frappé* is the *coupé* (to cut the weight), a push from the floor in *demi-plié* – a sharp impetus, the germ of lightness and lift.

Seventh, the **Rond de jambes par terre** and **en l'air** assist the turn-out and strengthening of the hip. *Rond de jambe par terre* in which the working leg describes a semi-circle on the floor, while the body remains motionless. *Rond de jambe en l'air* in which the working leg describes an oval to the side in quicker, lighter tempo. These movements contribute to the foundation of the *fouetté*.

Eighth, the **Développés** for forging the aesthetic line, making easy the unfolding of the leg into those high *écartés*, those *arabesques* and *attitudes* curving upwards, winglike – lines that speak of flight. Here is the whip-cord tension within the limb that vibrates a steel-like strength and lightness.

Ninth, the **Grands Battements** with upward accent, giving height and power – building a rhythmic dynamo.

Tenth, the **Petits battements** so light, so quick, so precise and airy – precursors of *batterie* and aerial momentum.

Eleventh, **Pliés-relevés** facing the *barre* – repetition of relax and stretch growing in tempo and fluidity.

Twelfth, the final stretching of the legs on the *barre*, the slow stretching of the ligaments releasing all tensions before work in the centre is attempted.

Epaulement – a misunderstood word that means so much. Perhaps this is the greatest secret of the school. The play of the shoulders and the head always falling in line with the body – the accomplishment that gives the longest line in every movement, and manifests a natural facility to turn, to play the bodily instrument with fluent delicacy.

The accomplishment bred on the *barre* is repeated in like order in the centre. The pattern is repeated unsupported, the practice continues, gathering momentum with growing orchestration of movement. This is the order of the day – of every day – yet each day the class is created anew: different combinations of steps, infinite variety of choreographic invention, as limitless as the harmony of notes in musical composition.

The discipline has to be tough since it has to toughen

sinews; but this discipline leads to the greatest freedom, and by its technique to the fullest expression. These few words about the sciences that conjure a perfection of movement are inadequate; they may only be considered as signposts.

The teachers' approach may be as variable as their personalities. Since the class is handed down from disciple to disciple there is no great discord in the doctrines taught. The quality of the teaching only differs by personal preference and application, and by the innate talent of the teacher. Thus the sequence of exercises varies slightly with individual teachers.

Observation and response: how to stand in first position.

Let us take a look at some of the classes operating today. One may see Irina Barshenova, a tall, dark girl with a beautiful instep and a firm grip, taking the first-year children – Kolpakova's daughter among them. The work at the *barre* takes a little over three-quarters of an hour. The accent is on thoroughness, a basic vocabulary articulated to slow rhythms, the stretch and the strength being consolidated in these soft young bodies with an insistent persuasiveness. The centre-work consists of *battements tendus, pliés* and *port de bras*, finishing with vertical jumps in the 1st position. At the conclusion the children march, trot and polka. They respond with a delightful spontaneity.

In a second-year class a more mature teacher, for whom teaching is an expression of motherly love, brings more subtle shadings. Her gentleness brings out poetry from the children's imaginations. After setting an *adage* entirely by gestures with her hands, she suddenly springs the command to improvise their own finishing position. Most of the children fall naturally into graceful and unusual poses, but one or two copy what their neighbours are doing.

The brilliant Tiuntina with a class of young boys is a lively experience – the atmosphere intense with youthful awe, and with feverish effort to succeed, to win approval from this demanding matriarch, who can crush with the ferocity of her bark. Other classes confirm the impression of strictness, firmness, of routine that must be accepted like a yoke until it becomes second-nature.

The ideal potential: a lightly boned body with soft resilient muscle texture and ligaments of supple elasticity.

In another studio a tired ballerina is teaching her flock with the same discipline with which she was treated half a century ago. She is without any visible evidence of her former glory; the frame that once was lithe and radiant is now heavy with the weight of years. There is a melting pathos when her crustiness evaporates and she unbends to give the merest hint of approval, bringing an expression of joy to the faces of these eager girls.

The class that Veniamin Zimin gives to the senior boys is a master class by any standards. Zimin is small and wiry, a creative teacher with the knowledge and artistry born of long experience. His class is full of invention, rhythm and beautiful movement – it is a performance. Zimin demonstrates with precision and grace; he is full of exuberance, at times too powerful for his pupils, who cannot always measure up to his demands.

In the little coaching theatre – which is a room with a raked stage and hanging spotlights, there are a few rows of seats for an audience. A large tank of a woman with straight bobbed hair is lambasting three long-haired youths who are attempting *tour en l'air* to the knee. She is a solid tower of strength, like a power station pumping energy into these lanky boys who leap and crumple, pick themselves up and fly into the air again. There is no music; but there is rhythm. This is a flurry of analysis and attack; the teacher's strategy, a blend of knowledge, co-ordination and muscle-power, dog-gedly breaking through barriers. There are pauses for breath, for summoning resources, and then a relentless driving on. They go at it again and again, by turns pleased and despondent, but continuously goaded by the sonorous voice of the teacher.

In contrast is the class of Serebriannikov, master of *pas de deux*. His quiet dignity extends to the pupils, who work with gentle but glowing enthusiasm. There is love in every movement – and what is *pas de deux* but the expression of harmony and love? Togetherness is taught – a felicity in every shade of feeling, in control and balance, in intertwining and evolving movements, and in aerial lifts. Action is preceded by explanation. First precise instruction, then the command followed by the placing of the hand, the hold on the hip, the manipulation like conjuring, the firm unflurried ease of *fouettés*, of turning and opening like a flower; maintaining equilibrium on the ground and in the air; the timing of ethereal lifts to a hair's breadth; all movement of two in one, intricate,

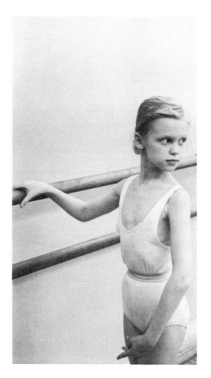

Eager beginnings.

65

Grands pliés *and* relevés.

Placing must come early.

sensitive, yet as spontaneous and simple as a sigh. 'Ne cto dela, no kak dela!' ('Not what you do, but how you do it!'). Serebriannikov is calm, aloof, explicit.

The effervescent Dudinskaya takes the graduating class. She carries tradition in her bones, but she is always looking ahead. A superb technician herself, she encourages her pupils to strive for greater power and skill. Dudinskaya is one of the principal guardians of the Classics. She has danced all the leading rôles, and can transmit every nuance of movement and musicality to the coming generations.

Madame has just returned from Cuba. Today she is late for class, a little travel-weary, but full of vigour. She is stern with her pupils, who may have slipped back a little during her absence. It is one of those days when everything seems just a little uneasy. A particularly unconquerable *enchaînement* is her exercise in the centre for double and triple *fouettés*. Nobody can quite master it, and a helpless impotence seems to freeze their desperate efforts. But the next *enchaînement*, a buoyant *allegro*, seems to unburden the dancers, and suddenly their execution becomes swift and sure. One little step has a Bournonville flavour. Dudinskaya's *grandes sautés* cover the large studio – a flying movement of great breadth that brings stylish responses from the awakened dancers.

Opposite, second year group.

Third year group.

Ballet cannot stand still – the technique of dance cannot flower without growth and development. Only fanaticism can transform bone and muscle into an image of grace that soars from the earth and seems to float magically.

The barre *is the scaffolding upon which the body is sculptured into an instrument of classical beauty.*

Second year boys.

The boys and girls rehearse a Quadrille. On the wall behind them is a portrait of the great ballerina Marina Semyonova.

Fourth year class-work.

Putting on pointe-*shoes.*

The joy and exhilaration of dancing on the pointe.

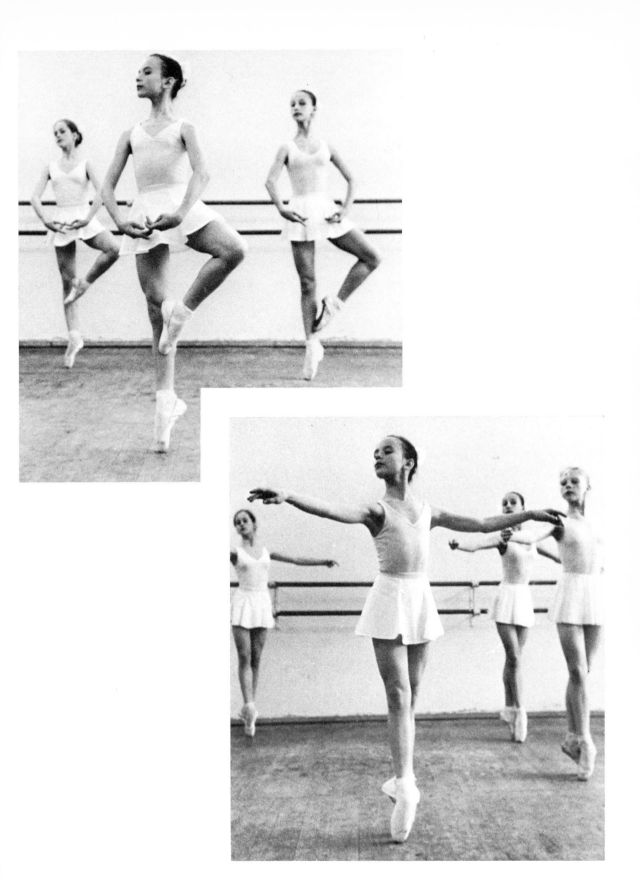

Fifth year class – togetherness in movement.

The grooming brings a harmony and lightness.

A sixth year group practise extensions at the barre *and show perfection of line in attitude.*

Graduate students in flight.

The elevation of *Vladimir Kim*.

Male prowess.

Pas de deux *class in action*.

Studies of Serebriannikov's pas de deux *class*.

Aspects of pas de deux.

The character barre – folk dance.

Russia and its neighbouring countries are rich in folk dance, and in the Leningrad school the rigidity of the classical concept has been softened by the rhythmic pulse and simple épaulement of this ethnic form of dance. There are no laws governing this interweaving of the simple and primitive with the artificial and sophisticated; the adaptation has been made with a sense of proportion and an aesthetic sense of fitness and ease.

ГОСУДАРСТВЕННЫЙ
ОРДЕНА ЛЕНИНА
АКАДЕМИЧЕСКИЙ

ТЕАТР ОПЕРЫ И БАЛЕТА

имени С.М.КИРОВА

ВСЕСОЮЗНЫЙ ФЕСТИВАЛЬ ИСКУССТВ
«БЕЛЫЕ НОЧИ»

196-й сезон

ВЫПУСКНОЙ СПЕКТАКЛЬ

Ленинградского академического
ордена Трудового Красного Знамени

ХОРЕОГРАФИЧЕСКОГО УЧИЛИЩА

имени нар. арт. РСФСР, профессора А. Я. Вагановой

Воскресенье, 24 июня 1979 г.

A Kirov Celebration

The Centenary of Agrippina Vaganova was celebrated by the dancers, teachers, and pupils of the Kirov during the White Nights Festival of 1979. Konstantine Sergeyev, assisted by Natalia Dudinskaya, produced for the occasion a special programme with pupils of the school, which was first given in the Grand Repetition Salle (a two-tier rehearsal hall specially constructed during the 1880s at the instigation of Ivan Vsevolodsky, director of The Imperial Theatre), in Rossi Street. The programme was later repeated for three gala performances at the Kirov.

Writing in the programme, Sergeyev expressed his belief that the contemporary school of classical ballet rested firmly upon the remarkable foundations of the traditional school, and his aim in creating these performances was to show the discipline and the creative processes of the choreographic system. Thus his programme opened with *Class Concert*, showing mixed grades of pupils performing the class exercises to the music of Drigo – remarkable music, Sergeyev affirmed, which has sustained the life of the Russian Ballet for many years, both in the class, and also in the repertoire of the classics.

In *Class Concert* the pupils gave a good account of themselves, with a high level of accomplishment, and a polished style. There were many endearing moments. A sensitive performance of *Chopiniana* followed, and the performance ended with a *Divertissement* in which the *grand pas de deux* from *Paquita* brought an exciting conclusion.

Vera Krasovskaya, Leningrad's historian of the ballet, wrote a glowing tribute.

'Agrippina Vaganova was taken into the Maryinsky corps de ballet in 1897, and her talent was soon recognised by the veteran choreographer Petipa. She became

Opposite, programme of the Vaganova centenary performance at the Kirov Theatre, Sunday, 24th June, 1979.

101

known to the critics as the "Queen of Variations", so brilliant were her solos in *Coppélia, Don Quixote* and *The Little Hump-backed Horse*.

Just before the Revolution Vaganova left the stage and took up teaching. For a time she taught in A. L. Volinsky's private school of Russian Ballet, but later transferred to the State school. From 1921 she taught the last three finishing classes in the Leningrad Choreographic Academy, which some years later was named after her. From her teaching emerged a string of brilliant ballerinas. The first, in 1925, was Marina Semeonova, a ballerina of great depth and eloquence whose inspired dancing reaffirmed the unfading traditions of the Russian Ballet. There followed others of different personalities and talents, but all had the superb mastery of the Vaganova schooling. Olga Jordan was like a flame, brilliant and flowing; Galina Ulanova brought a new wonder, revealing unrealised depths in old rôles, and creating new images in new ballets. Tatiana Vetcheslova with her histrionic gifts reached the heights in comedy and dramatic parts. Natalia Dudinskaya, the most beloved of Vaganova's pupils, became the "star" of Leningrad's scene; besides excelling in the traditional ballets, she created many rôles in the modern repertoire. Alla Shelest was an actor-dancer who could impart the most subtle psychological nuances.

Every spring brought forth a new ballerina of surpassing brilliance. In 1950 Alla Osipenko finished school. Her refined beauty of line had no equal. In 1951 the last of Vaganova's pupils appeared: Irina Kolpakova, a refined and beautiful dancer, whose light still radiates in our time.'

From 1931 to 1937 Vaganova held the position of Artistic Director of the Kirov Ballet. During this period she staged her versions of *Swan Lake* and *Esmeralda,* while Vainonen staged his *Flames of Paris* and Zakharov produced *The Fountain of Bakhchiserai* to the music of Asafiev. These ballets are now considered to be living classics of the Soviet Ballet of the 'thirties.

At a special gathering in the Grand Repetition Salle in the school during the White Nights Festival, guests of honour were Marina Semeonova, Tatiana Vetcheslova and Natalia Dudinskaya, all of whom spoke of their personal reminiscences of Vaganova, and Sergeyev gave an impassioned speech in which he emphasized that the traditions of Vaganova are still alive today.

Tatiana Ariskina and Artur Avdalyan in the pas de deux *from* Chopiniana.

Boys rehearse for the Vaganova Celebration.

Rehearsal of Chopiniana.

Islo Ganyeva and Artur Avdalyan rehearsing pas de deux.

Boys rehearsing demonstration class for the Vaganova Celebration.

Class Concert *on stage at the Kirov Theatre.*

Façade, auditorium and drop-curtain of the Kirov Theatre.

On Stage at the Kirov

'. . . Leonardo da Vinci was in sympathy with the rendering of movement through style . . . He felt that movement to be perpetuated in art must be of a special kind. It must be a visible expression of grace.

. . . Although Renaissance writers left no formal definition of that word grace, they would all have agreed that it implied a series of smooth transitions. It was to be found perfectly exemplified in flowing gestures, floating draperies, curling or rippling hair. An abrupt transition was brutal; the graceful was continuous.'

Sir Kenneth Clark,
Leonardo da Vinci.

*Opposite, frescoed ceiling of the Kirov.
Below, the dancers prepare.*

Today the Kirov enters the technological age with a lively step, offering super-dancers who appear to be powered by nuclear energy! Those qualities of lyricism and grace are still there, but with a sharpened edge; a new brittle modernism predominates. The dancer is of our time. There may be differing opinions about costumes and scenery, about choreographic content and invention, but there are no two opinions about the Kirov dancers; whether at home or abroad, they lead the way. The proof of their superiority is contained in this book; it is stated in the history and long tradition of the school and company. By comparison Western Ballet is still young, perhaps now in the vigorous age of adolescence.

At home in stately Leningrad the new dancers shine in the old setting. Life goes on in the old way – the morning matinées, the benefit galas, the revivals, the premières; fashions change but not the fundamentals. The core of truth and greatness is held firm in the permanent frame of the school and the theatre. Together they form an absolute unity to maintain discipline, integrity and beauty, cardinal principles that must never be lost.

Such is the vigour, the strength and the love – there is never any apparent staleness. Whether old masters, or new pieces, all works of art are kept in a state of meticulous repair; they are polished and preserved with scrupulous care, they are danced with every fibre of the dancers' being, with *élan*.

Days and nights filled with Kirov ballet are lively and stimulating. Getting up in the dark, crossing the frozen Neva, traversing those cheerless streets in the grey gloom to the glorious warmth and elegance of the Kirov Theatre! Cinderella at 11.30 in the morning might be a daunting prospect; but in fact it is enchanting, although Prokofiev's restless music might seem unsatisfactory for this ballet. It is perhaps too involved and refractory. But Sergeyev's ballet is brilliantly contrived; the production is highly polished, the *mise-en-scène* excellent, the corps de ballet finely drilled, and the children excel in their delightful appearances – like little professionals. Everything is as it should be; but the greatest joy is Svetlana Efremova as Cinderella – an entrantingly beautiful girl with winsome charm and lithe speed. One moment she tears the heart-strings with the pathos of her acting, the next she is electrifying; her *batterie* deceives the eye; the speed of her *manège* is baffling. She is all magic!

And in those June days that have no nights there is the

Opposite, Svetlana Efremova as Cinderella.

117

annual Festival of the White Nights, when numerous galas are given. *Hamlet* takes the stage! Sergeyev's interpretation of Shakespeare's masterpiece must rank amongst the great epic ballets. It is the homogeneous conception of a team: Sergeyev, choreographer, Tchervinsky, composer, Yunovitch, designer.

Konstantine Sergeyev said: 'The most difficult thing in ballet is to find a form of movement which would suit the internal spirit of the image. The dance material should find its development in accordance with the growth of the dramatic image and in strict alliance with the musical pattern.' With his production of *Hamlet* Sergeyev has carried out his precepts in a masterly way.

Konstantine Sergeyev rehearsing Nikita Dolgushin in the part of Hamlet.

Opposite, Nikita Dolgushin as Hamlet.

Above, Nikita Dolgushin; right, Elena Evteyeva as Ophelia and A. Mironov as Polonius; below, after the play scene.

Svetlana Efremova as Ophelia and Vadim Budharin as Laertes; Elena Evteyeva as Ophelia.

Left, Anatole Sapogov rehearsing Claudius; below, Dolgushin as Hamlet with Gabriel Komleva as Ophelia; opposite, Anatole Sapogov as Claudius with Olga Moiseyeva as Gertrude.

Giselle, the most loved of all Romantic ballets, has sometimes been called the Hamlet of the ballet – doubtless because of its great dramatic rôle for the ballerina. At the Kirov it is continuously in the repertoire, with numerous interpretations. For some years the rôles of Giselle and Albrecht have been taken by Irina Kolpakova and Yuri Soloviev, and no more lyrical portrayal of these parts could ever have been given. Tragically, Soloviev has passed from the scene, but Kolpakova remains a queen among ballerinas, still shining in the classical repertoire.

Left, Galina Ulanova as Giselle; below and opposite, Irina Kolpakova as Giselle, Serge Vikulov as Albrecht, G. Selyutsky as Hilarion.

The production of *Giselle* is so meticulously thought out that not a moment lacks eloquence, and at the same time all unnecessary distractions have been omitted. This is the tragic-romantic story wrought with simplicity and beauty. Unobtrusively, traps are used to enable the Queen of the Willis to appear like an apparition out of the ground, and in the same manner Giselle appears from the grave and returns to the grave. The effect adds to the magic.

The whole production is a monument to inspired teamwork, in which Vladimir Fedotov, the conductor, and his orchestra must take chief honours. Fedotov has almost recomposed Adam's music. His rendering is so integrated with the nature of the action as to be synonymous with it. He is a genius who can handle *rubato* with a thousand shades; the effect in the mad scene is spell-binding. It is this total musicality, a marriage of music and movement, that renders the Leningrad Ballet homogeneous and perfect.

Scenes from the second act of Giselle: *Irina Kolpakova and Serge Vikulov together with corps de ballet.*

The saga of *Swan Lake* continues – the test of ballerina-
dom! In the Second Act how exquisite is that nymph from
Perm, Lubov Konakova. Her frail beauty, her solitary
dedication . . . yet as Odile she can turn the scales with mocking and lascivious treachery. In these rôles Valentina Hannebalova from Tbilisi is of a different breed; dark, shining,
beautifully proportioned, her lyrical and dramatic power is
unassailable.

Opposite and right, scenes from the second act of Swan Lake; *below, Valentina Hannebalova and Serge Vikulov in scene from the third act.*

For the most part the atmosphere of Russian classical ballet is potent and heady with the music of Russian composers; its sweetness and sensuous cadences seduce the senses like a drug. The richness of Glazunov, the luscious texture of sound he has given to *Raymonda*, creates the enchanted world. In this ballet the mercurial Gabriella Komleva exercises her wizardry; and the chemistry of her personality allied to her technical mastery weaves a spell. Her absolute freedom and effortlessness reflect the traditional glory of the school. But we may see her equally at ease in the contemporary style of *The Path of Thunder*.

Undoubtedly there are ballets in the repertoire that have outlived their time – ballets that creak with age. Yet these concoctions of Minkus and Pugni and Drigo, these old ballets – *Paquita, Bayadère, Harlequin* – so loved and cherished, can be seen over and over again, with old and new ballerinas, and all

are acceptable in presentation despite the quaint ambiguities, musical and literary. The incredible *Faust Bacchanalia* of Gounod with its particular brand of Russian coyness – those satyrs of mocking profanity whose sensual exploits tease and thrill – is a fascinating diversion, deliciously sensuous and vulgar.

Then there is the archaic *Fountain of Bakhchiserai*, poetic and crude, spiritual and primitive ... Zakharov's melodramatic epic of Pushkin's immortal tale set to Asafiev's lurid melodies. But it brings from obscurity the elfin Alla Sizova, symbol of purity, to be woo'd by the tireless Gennady Selyutsky – or the dauntless Ninel Kurgapkina, ageless and prim, firm as a silken wire, sparkling with the cold brilliance of a diamond. There are countless Marias, but always the mind goes back to the wan fragrance of Ulanova, the original Maria, who made this tale as sad and moving as Pushkin's romantic tragedy.

Scenes from Raymonda: *Kolpakova with Vikulov (opposite) and with Oleg Sokolov (above left).*

Scenes from Paquita *with corps de ballet.*

Opposite, Kirov auditorium at interval time.

Valentina Hannebalova in Walpurgis Night.

Above and opposite, Bacchantes.

To excite and thrill there are the virile leaps of such notable dancers as Anatole Pavlovsky. These are phenomenal expositions of dance that seem to defy Nature's laws, when the spirit takes over and carries muscle and sinew into the realm of mystical and unchartered forces. One can but look on and marvel, and feel the exhilaration of the spirit.

Alexander Pavlovsky as Nuraly in The Fountain of Bakhchiserai.

To miss a morning with *Don Quixote* is to miss a rare treat. This pseudo-Spanish pot pourri with Minkus at his most extravagant joyously offers a romping display of dancing that by its sheer infectious gaiety and abandon is simply enthralling. The Kitri of Valentina Hannebalova brings such a display of fireworks – she and her partner, the handsome Vadim Budharin, sail through the ballet as if it were a frolic for their own amusement – a note taken up by the whole company so that it becomes a carnival *par excellence* enjoyed by performers and audience in like measure.

Another memorable revival was *The Nutcracker* in the Vainonen version, re-staged by Sergeyev for the school. This Nutcracker had all the period charm of a Victorian Christmas party in St. Petersburg. The excitement of the children, the mystery of Drosselmeyer, the puppets, the magic, the exuberance of the rats and the Kingdom of Sweets unfolded as a romantic dream should, in graceful harmony. In this lavish and elegant production two graduates from the school made their Kirov début, and Elena Vorontzova and Eugene Kalinov gave proof that the future is not without promise.

Alla Sizova as Maria.

139

Opposite, Elena Evteyeva as Kitri.

Right, Svetlana Efremova and Mikhail Baryshnikov as Kitri and Basil.

Below, Vladimir Ponemarev as Don Quixote.

It is impossible in this eulogy of dancers to forget the fragrance of Elena Evteyeva. A beautifully-moulded creature, like a young Karsavina, her soul speaks through her infinitely graceful movement. In *Chopiniana* she carries a melting sadness, she is the Sylph transcendent . . . In *Hamlet* her Ophelia is a wraith, wistful, forlorn . . . In *Creation of the World* she is another creature, of the earth, her body bending like a willow to Nature's contortions, an instrument that plays in the wind; in *Leningrad Symphony* she is a human soul racked with sorrow. All shades of feeling are encompassed in the poetry of her movement. She is a quiet creature, ever composed, ever unruffled . . .

Memorable, too, are Alla Osipenko and her husband, the magnificent Johnnie Markovsky. No longer members of the Kirov, they nevertheless are children of the Kirov. Their half-hour-long *pas de deux* giving an interpretation of Antony and Cleopatra in concert performances is a work in a contemporary style of movement, astringent, acrobatic and powerful in intensity. It is a vehicle that enables Osipenko to exhibit her full range and rouse her audiences to vociferous hysteria.

Entr'acte.

Irina Kolpakova in pas de cinq *from* The Nutcracker.

Opposite, Galina Ulanova in Chopiniana (Les Sylphides). *No dancer has ever excelled the floating grace of Ulanova in this ballet. There exists a fragment of film which has captured for posterity the rare quality of this artist in the* pas de deux. *Below, corps de ballet in* Chopiniana.

Scenes from Chopiniana.

Above, Natalia Bolshakova and Vadim Gulyayev in Creation of the World.

Left, Yuri Soloviev as God.

Opposite above, Evteyeva as Eve, Breznoi as Adam.

Opposite below, Bolshakova and Gulyayev.

Two studies of Irina Kolpakova and Yuri Soloviev in The Sleeping Beauty.

Opposite above, Alla Sizova as Prin-cess Aurora.

Opposite below, Elena Evteyeva and L. Kovalev in the Bluebird pas de deux.

Svetlana Efremova as Princess Aurora and Serge Vikulov as Prince Flori-munde.

Left, Lubov Konakova as the Lilac
Fairy.

Below, Elena Alexeyeva as the Pussy-
cat.

Opposite, Irina Kolpakova as Princess
Aurora.

156

Opposite, Galina Ulanova – the original Juliet in Lavrovsky's production of Romeo and Juliet.

Right and below, Irina Kolpakova and Yuri Soloviev as the tragic lovers.

Scenes from Antony and Cleopatra *with Alla Osipenko and John Markovsky. (Ballet produced for independent touring group.)*

Moments of elevation from the ballet Laurencia.

Svetlana Efremova in Levsha (Left-handed Man) *with L. Kovmir.*

164

More studies of Efremova and Kovmir in Levsha.

More studies of Efremova and Kovmir in Levsha.

Overleaf, eight studies of Konstantin Rossadin as Severyan in The Stone Flower.

Scene in the underground kingdom from The Stone Flower *with Alla Osipenko as Mistress of the Stone Mountain.*

Thus continue the triumphs of the Kirov's dancers of today; some who are no longer young, some who are coming into maturity, and some who are on the way. What is evident and reassuring is the sanguine and intrepid continuity of the school. The Cradle of Ballet rocks, joyfully maintaining its momentum of creative effort and producing a level of art that is never less than miraculous.

This miracle of physical accomplishment is worked upon an old (some might say, worn-out) repertoire of classical masterpieces that has been patched and repatched, forever refurbished, countless times retold, and reappearing always with a freshness and a pristine splendour that invigorates the senses. This conglomerate repertoire is the superstructure and the means by which the dancers exercise their power. These classics of the last century with all their incongruities are accepted without criticism or ridicule; they have acquired a unanimous respect, and their absurdities have been made acceptable by their interpreters. They are the magician's means! One accepts ballet as one accepts fantasy, with gratitude and joy in the escape it offers from the reality and stress of ordinary life.

A classic is a classic in any period; it has a permanence by reason of its virtue, its poetic truth, its living animation. This tarnished repertoire outmoded by time and fashion is still cogent; it relates to human nature, to the heart of man. Leningrad keeps this treasure alive and vital.

Epilogue

Backstage at the Kirov one feels lost in the maze of winding corridors and passages which give off to countless offices, workshops, rehearsal rooms, canteen, dressing-rooms, wardrobe and so on. There is no luxury and no permanency of tenure for the artisans who labour here; dressing-rooms have to be shared with the Opera and vacated after each performance. The lay-out has been modernized and enlarged, but the heavily glazed yellow walls and the reddish-brown tiles speak of age. The atmosphere is as cold and impersonal as a barracks, but in winter the temperature is like a hot-house. It must have been very cramped in Tzarist times, but today there is more space.

The stage is heavily raked and gloomy in the half-light before rehearsal begins. Dancers come and go while stage-hands talk in quiet groups. Kovmir is practising his beats to Fedotov's silent conducting. Other dancers are going through the motions in dark corners; some sweat at perfecting fragments of dance.

The set is a new décor for *Giselle*. It looks rather ordinary. The fairy castle that dominated Benois's backcloth, and which inspired so many more, has disappeared, and in its place is a vague turreted building that looks more like an abbey. The auditorium is swathed in white dust-sheets, its glory hidden by mantles that in the dim greyness give the impression of snow. Musicians are assembling in the pit, and tuning noisily. The hubbub grows into a bedlam until Fedotov, silver-haired and distinguished, stills the cacophany with one sweep of the hand. The drop-cloth is lowered, the overture begins. Another *Giselle* with Mendsentsova and Zaklinsky. . . .

At this morning's rehearsal disappointment prevails. Vinogradov, the new director, has endeavoured to bring a new look to an old work, but this *Giselle* has not the magic of

Opposite, Olga Chenchikova in Paquita.

the well-loved production it supplants. Refurbishing has not been stinted; there are louder costumes, flying willis; but no 'traps' and no mystery. The *Giselle* of old was simple, poetic, musical; this one is laboured and pedestrian. It has no magic.

There must be change, experiments. The new director has problems. How to bridge the old with the new; how to progress and develop? With the enthusiastic first flush a clean sweep has been made – but enthusiasm may sometimes destroy what would be better left untouched.

Vinogradov has brought Roland Petit from Paris to produce his *Hunchback of Notre Dame*, a work whose choreographic style is more akin to physical jerks than the aesthetics of classical dance. Yet with what relish the Kirov dancers tackle the new medium! It freshens them and sends them throbbing into action, but in this work their highly tuned bodies are scarcely called upon to express their range.

How can the Kirov maintain its continuity of style? It looks as though Vinogradov and his predecessor, Sergeyev, are at loggerheads in their outlook as once were Fokine and Legat – the eternal struggle to hold fast to tradition is in conflict with the urge to seek new paths. The quality of productions will be likely to vary, as will the talent from the school: it is as the fluctuation of seasons – the ebb and flow of tides – the swing of the pendulum.

During the last war, when the school and company was evacuated to Perm in the Urals, a new grafting was effected and the fine plant of the Kirov strain took root and was cross-fertilized in a new nursery. Today in Perm, Ludmilla Zakharova, a teacher who dates from that period, is producing a new line of ballerinas, possibly the ballerina assoluta of our time. Her first outstanding pupil was the brilliant Nadia Pavlova, winner of the gold medal at the Moscow International Ballet competition, who was immediately snapped up by the Bolshoi Ballet and raised to stardom.

Zakharova appears to be able to select a particular talent and cultivate it to a state of perfection that seems almost miraculous. Her ballerinas are elegant, finely tempered, they appear to be equipped with inner dynamos that enhance the quality of their movements with a hidden strength, and enable them to execute flashes of brilliance with unruffled assurance. Her dancers have a technical superiority and beauty of movement that are phenomenal. Her two girls, Lubov Konakova and Olga Chinchikova, bring a new strength to the Kirov's present period of uncertainty

In the last analysis, the Kirov Ballet – like Russia itself – is enigmatic and unpredictable. Just when things seem to have reached a state of stagnation or instability, some mystical guidance will inspire the fervent troupe suddenly to excel itself by staging a ravishing revival that will leave the audience breathless with wonder. Such an occasion was the Gala Concert of the White Nights Festival of 1978, which opened quietly with a restrained performance of *Chopiniana* (*Les Sylphides*), included a faithful rendering of Anton Dolin's *Pas de Quatre*, and ended with a sumptuous staging of the refurbished *Paquita divertissement*.

Re-staged under the consultative guidance of veteran Pyotr Gusev, the venerable director of the Conservatoire, almost every teacher of note would appear to have had a hand in the production, including Dudinskaya, Tiuntina, Okhova, Kurgapkina, Legat, Koneshev and Semenov.

Even the backcloth was a masterpiece, and drew applause before the dancers entered. It was a gravura impression of the Kirov auditorium seen from the stage – an auditorium filled with Imperial splendour. And then – a stunning surprise, and for no other reason than that they are beautiful and truly Russian – the children from the school dashed on in the Suvorovtsy Quadrille. Glamorously attired in white and gold, they danced with such style and aplomb that the audience went wild before the ballet had even begun.

After this explosion the corps de ballet entered like shining jewels and a feast of dancing ensued. What magnificence! It was as though the clock had been turned back some seventy years . . . but the stage was peopled with a new race of dancers who revived the spirit of Petipa . . . The cast was headed by Chenchikova and Breznoi, together with Iskanderova, Sollun, Sizova, Konakova, Hannebalova and Lupokova. The variations were performed with a passionate intensity that overrode all flaws, with a joyous virtuosity that surpassed the boundaries of human skill. That old Kirov magic had taken the stage once more, and with such abundance! Dances that had been laid away in the dust of years took the stage with a fresh *élan*. Nothing had been spared to make this *Paquita* memorable.

Yesterday there were some lamentations about the new *Giselle*, the day before there were some misgivings, but now, with *Paquita* reborn, all is bliss . . .

Curtain-call.

Irina Kolpakova.

'*And when the curtain falls
may there be flowers*'

John Masefield

PRODUCTIONS FROM WHICH PHOTOGRAPHS
HAVE BEEN SELECTED